AMBER DICKSON

Nasty Billionaire Daddy

A Thrilling Age Gap, Friends With Benefits Erotic Romance

Contents

Chapter 1

Ashley Gray loved everything sex-related. She loved the toe-curling feel of having someone pound into her relentlessly and eat her out like she was some rare delicacy. She also loved the slow fucking. The kind that made you forget your name which was why she loved having Ethan around.

Ethan Jefferson, a multi-billionaire, with baby blue eyes, dark hair, and tall with a lean muscular physique, was her friend with benefit. They were both insanely physically attracted to each other, but Ashley wasn't looking for anything serious just yet. And Ethan was more than fine with it, hence, their agreement to keep fooling around and having mind-blowing sex.

Currently, he was in her apartment. They had sex the night before and he had slept over. She managed to turn away from him in her sleepy tossing, only to be mildly startled by his unconscious motion to spoon her body. Her senses were more alert at that precise moment.

Ashley was reminded of their physical characteristics—tall, strong, and interwoven within one another—by the heat exchanged between their bodies. The innocence of the scenario started to draw her into a foggy imagination of not-so-innocent thoughts as she felt his limp cock against her ass cheeks. She continued to press her ass against him for a brief period to test whether it would be sufficient to awaken him.

Though Ethan was still mostly sleeping, the action roused him enough for him to slide his palm up her inner leg from her knee, prompting her to consider waking them up. So that his fingers were resting against the top of her clit, she moved his hand to her panties. He realized where his body parts had fallen as he began to wake up. He pushed her thighs apart to make sure of her intentions and see if she would respond. She did.

He firmly gripped her hips and pulled them closer to him as his hand moved away from the top of her panties. She gasped slightly at the same time. He was aware that the thought of fucking her sideways drove her nuts. His hand returned to her underwear after he asserted that her body would be taken care of that night.

Already wet, she was. He traced his middle finger slowly from the top of her panties all the way down to her pussy.

"Mmmm...Ethan," she moaned. She could see stars even in the pitch black.

Ashley adjusted her body so that her back was flush with the mattress and guided his fingers underneath the waist of her panties as he began to rub. As he first touched her wet pussy that morning, it allowed her to open her thighs. She could feel a drop of precum on the light cotton that was restricting his cock as she grabbed it, which was rigidly pitching a tent in his boxers.

"You want more?" Ethan asked in his insanely sexy husky voice.

"Yes, please," she panted.

He inserted one finger into her pussy as she attempted to grab under his waistband. She couldn't help but bury her head in the pillow once more. It was far superior to a fantasy. Even though they weren't saying anything, their bodies were making a lot of noise that could be heard. The pace of their savoring each other increased. She could feel his cock already pulsing in her hand as he occasionally slipped his fingers out to rub her clit with the moisture of her hole.

She flipped over and holding his cock tightly in her hand, slowly rubbed it from the top of her clit to the rim of her asshole to ensure that the tip was covered in pussy fluid.

"Shit," he cursed.

He could no longer take it. He stopped at her pussy hole to chastise her by grabbing hold of his cock and rubbing it against her clit. She could no longer bear it at this point. She backed up her ass the next time he tried to tease her, allowing his cock to slide into her warm pussy.

With each deeper thrust, they both let out a shrill scream and continued to take deep breaths. As he penetrated her from behind, he reached around and continued to rub her clit to ensure that she was also taken care of.

"Oh my god, Ethan!" She couldn't help but sink her fingers into his forearm as it continued for a few more intensifying minutes. She let go of the pressure to move her hand over his to feel him rub her clit when she suddenly realized how tightly she was holding him.

She realized that they hadn't even kissed when he kissed the back of her shoulder up along her neck. As she turned her head and moved closer to his lips, they brushed against each other's tongues. He started to fuck her harder as the intensity of their kissing increased.

"Ahh!" she cried out completely in a haze.

Because of the pleasure which was making her scream, she was unable to reciprocate his kisses.

Her orgasm was edging closer as he completely indulged in her pleasure. He was well aware of this, so he moved his hand underneath her lacy nightgown and extended it to play with both of her nipples simultaneously. Her pussy was stuffed and ready for ecstasy, and her nipples were already hard. He slowed his fuck to feel her muscles tighten around his thickening cock as she climaxed, and pulsed throughout her entire body. She was sure she had made it to the earthly heavens. As her pussy continued to contract, he was unable to hold back and pumped faster.

He quickly pulled out his cock to cum all over her bare ass. She kissed him as he continued to pulsate.

"Good morning, Ashley," he said once he was able to catch his breath.

"What a way to begin the day." she smiled blissfully, slipping out of bed naked.

"As sexy as always," Ethan praised and she smirked.

"Flattery would get you everywhere," she said, going back to plant a kiss on his lips. "Now, get up, and let's shower. I need to be at work and you need to be at the office."

He groaned. "I believe being the CEO gives me the liberty to go to work whenever the hell I want."

Ashley grinned and shook her head. "No, it doesn't. You have a meeting with some Chinese investors, remember?"

His eyes widened. "Oh, shit!"

With the speed of lightning, he bolted out of bed into the shower and Ashley chuckled.

Silly hot moronic Ethan.

Chapter 2

"Hi!" Suzie, Ashley's friend squealed when she opened the door and engulfed her in a bear hug.

"I missed you too. Now, can you let me go? I can't breathe," Ashley forced out and Suzie freed her from her death-like grip.

"Oh don't be silly. I missed you," she pouted.

"I missed you too," Ashley replied, shutting the door as her friend sauntered into her apartment, looking like the goddess she was.

Both friends had similar features. Strawberry blonde hair, five-six height, and curvy hips. But where her eyes were coffee brown, Suzie's were azure. They had been best friends since high school and Ashley loved her like a sister. Whenever she felt down or heartbroken, Suzie was always there to assure her that everything was going to be alright.

"I brought chocolate chip cookies," Suzie said, placing the box on the coffee table and taking a piece for herself.

Ashley chuckled, plopping next to her best friend on the couch. "Well, thank you."

"I barely see you these days. Is Ethan's dick that good that you forget you have a best friend?"

It wasn't as bad as Suzie was making it sound. They usually spoke from time to time.

"You're being dramatic."

"Am I now? What's the deal with you and him anyways? Still fuck buddies?"

"Yup."

Suzie smirked. "Then his dick must really be good for you guys to be doing this for what? How long has it been?"

Ashley knew Suzie knew exactly how long it'd been. She was only teasing her.

"Three months."

"No strings attached?" her brow was arched.

"None whatsoever. Why are you asking?"

She shrugged. "Just curious. I don't see how you can fuck someone for three months straight and not have an atom of feeling for them. He seems like a decent guy though but just be cautious, okay?"

Ashley appreciated Suzie looking out for her which was why several moments later after she had left, she found herself thinking about what she had said.

* * *

Ethan called later that evening and asked if he could come over and she agreed. When he arrived, he looked exhausted, yet pant-droppingly gorgeous.

"How did the meeting go?" she asked, pouring him a glass of wine.

He sighed. "It went well. I'm just so tired from all the paperwork and stuff. How did your day go?" he asked as she sat on his lap, her own glass in her hand.

"Well, all things considered, it was good."

She observed him. "Should I help you relax?"

"By all means yes," he replied eagerly.

Ashley's thumb stroked the back of his knuckles gently. She then began to kiss him after dropping their glasses on the table. Her tongue caressed his.

As she drew back, she ran her index finger down his face and continued to run her hand down his arm. She slipped off his lap with a cheeky smile on her face. That smile had turned into a wide grin. She crept up his legs and went straight for his zipper.

Her gaze was drawn to Ethan's dick, and she sank back down between his legs, clutching it firmly. She ran her tongue from his balls up the length of his cock, whirled her tongue around his frenulum, pausing to lick the assembling cum, and then eagerly took him into her mouth after encircling his frenulum and dragging her tongue along the length of his cock, starting at his balls.

"Fuck, baby. Just like that," he groaned in approval.

"Mmm…" She thrust her head slightly.

She made no mistake about how to tease that special region right below his tip with her focused tongue and firm lips. She seemed to be enjoying herself, and Ethan could tell by her exuberance. She then started working on his cock as carefully as if it were the nicest ice cream.

She saw his hardening and the nearness of his orgasm, so she stood up and kissed him. She pushed her tongue pretty far into his mouth while grinning eagerly. It was quite evident that she was to give and he was to receive.

She then took her breasts out of her lacy bra and wanked him in her cleavage. Her knowledge was so obviously evident. Knowing that pressure was key, she massaged him against her warm chest while pressing her tits together.

"Ahh..shit!"

She moved down again, taking him again into her lips. Her head moved in a variety of ways—rapid bobbing, harder, slower nods—but she never wavered in her focus on his frenulum. As if an elastic band was connected from that point to the tip of her tongue, she was constantly drawn back to that area of sexual fulfillment.

She gave his balls a moment of her full attention, sucking and squeezing them into her mouth before spitting them out and shifting her attention back to his shaft.

He was going to blow. "I'm going to cum," he breathed.

As she gave him a passionate kiss, he felt his need intensify as he tasted his own tang on her tongue.

He saw Ashley had a gleam in her eye that suggested she wanted him to cum as she returned to lick his cock and suck his balls. Her head movements became more aggressive, her lips tightened, and her slurping became louder as pre-cum and saliva coated his cock.

She then started wanking him hard.

The last act, the conclusion.

She would soon feel his orgasm. Her hold on him became more firm with each thrust as she continued to pump quickly.

As her eyes were fixated on him and her tongue was prepared to grab him, he felt an inner release. She made sure she swallowed all of his precious liquid goodness as soon as the first precious drips of his cum appeared.

Ethan simply adored it whenever a woman marked a climax.

Every drop of his cum was sucked out through a series of rapid licks. Never before had he been milked in such a delightful, thorough, or skilled manner.

Before taking one last sip of her wine, Ashley gave a sly grin. She rested her head on his chest.

"How do you feel after that?" she asked, a sly smile still on her full lips.

"Much better, babe. I want to return the favor," he said, rubbing her thigh but she declined his offer.

"Not now. You're clearly stressed."

Chapter 3

Ethan invited Ashley over to a work party as his date and she was a little bit skeptical about going. Did being friends with benefits entail going to dinner parties as a couple?

Sitting in front of her dresser, she applied her makeup, and not too long after, the doorbell rang. It was no doubt Ethan coming to pick her up.

When she opened the door, the sight that greeted her was outer worldly. He was stunning. Breathtakingly handsome and for a moment she forgot how to speak.

"Wow," he exclaimed as his gaze swept over her in the most salacious once over. His orbs hooded with lust. "You look brilliant," he said in awe and she shook her head to clear it.

"You look dashing yourself."

"How am I supposed to keep my eyes off you at the party and concentrate?"

She smirked. "You're not supposed to keep your eyes off me at all, Mr. Jefferson."

Ethan cursed under his breath. He was turned on. Hot for her. But they were late so they exited her apartment.

As she drank at the party later that evening, savoring the softly fizzing bubbles popping on her tongue, she took in Ethan's image. Like all the men present, he was scrubbed up. But he, in particular, had perfected a sophisticated look and was devastatingly handsome in his tuxedo.

Not long after he was done talking to his business associates, they found a closet. She pushed her body in his direction to signal approval as he drew closer and started running his fingers up her thighs. He raised his hands, and she extended her legs, allowing him to journey all the way to her black underwear and press his hands into her oozing pussy. Even though they were completely alone in the little, well-kept enclosure, the idea that someone might find them, interrupt, and catch them was exhilarating. She decided that she didn't care because she didn't really know anyone there. Being discovered was well worth the thrill.

His tender yet firm and masterful lips continued to push against hers as they passionately kissed, and his tongue explored and teased her. He gazed with wide-eyed delight as she swayed her hips and thrust herself onto his fingers wantonly. As she swiftly released him, her hand slid down his body and began stroking his cock through his pants. His gasp could be heard.

"Fuck, baby."

She took his dick in her hand and began deliberately wanking his shaft before speeding up. While moving her black sequined dress out of the way, he continued to finger her cunt. Their intense fervor only got stronger.

"Yes, yes, I'm so wet now, could you please fuck me?"She began to pant into his cock, dazed.

"You want me to fuck you, dirty girl?" he asked and she nodded eagerly. "I want to hear you beg for my cock."

"Please fuck me, daddy. Please." she batted her lashes at him. If there was anything Ethan loved, it was being called daddy.

He didn't require any more incentive. Ashley was turned over by Ethan, who then dragged her now wet panties down. He rammed his dick home with one slam, wrenching her gaping, glistening wet hole. As he continued to ride her deeply from behind, she let out a loud cry.

"Shit! Just like that, daddy. Fuck!"

The cold, hardness of the marble table caused her knees to rub against it. He nudged her away; She held more tightly, turning her knuckles white. As a symbol of her filthy fucking, she liked combat wounds, so a friction burn wouldn't be a problem; Like a slut with a strut, she would wear it with pride.

The carefully placed pins fell out and her long hair dangled free. As she firmly gripped the table's edge, it scattered all over her face and back. Their fucking was shockingly full, bestial, and desperate. She had to compel herself to breathe into the fierce, inundating sensations and see black spots and stars within herself because it almost hurt.

She yelled, gasping, "Oh my *god!*"

"You like that hmm? My cock ramming into your tight little pussy? Yeah, take it, baby. Take daddy's massive cock."

She stimulatingly pulled her own ass cheeks open as she reached around, holding onto her ass, allowing for extra pounding. She wondered how they could have attained such a tremendous frenetic stride in such a short amount of time as they bounced together and he reacted flawlessly.

He thrust her body into him hungrily, still with such frantic longing, just as she reached a crescendo and was about to kiss him. He intuitively knew how to extend her shivering joy. He fell to his knees and extravagantly lapped her slick hole, savoring her creamy orgasmic juices and exhilarating her pulsing button. She drew his head closer to her, and she was swept away by pools of exquisite magic.

He quickly stood up, gave her a brief kiss, and then fucked her once more on her back, this time with one leg suspended in the air. He saw her overcome with an agonizing pleasure. The expanded view of his cock penetrating her made him smile.

"You're amazing, baby,"Ethan breathed and jerked his head back with complete sexual abandon.

While he continued to fuck her mercilessly like a man on a mission, she licked her fingers and played frantically with her sensitized clit. As he entered her, her fingers slipped down and encircled his cock. He was almost going to cum due to the vigor. His taught body trembled and the pressure that was growing in his face was apparent to her. He halted, pulled out, and dug his face into her worn-out clit. She rocked into his face as she held his head and rocked back in pure bliss.

"Ohhhh, fuck that feels so great!"She gasped.

"Your turn, dirty girl, take daddy's cock in your pretty little mouth and suck."

He got up and gently pushed her to her knees. She took his rock-hard cock in her hand and began sucking and stroking him as well as lovingly kissing and licking his balls, first slowly and then more quickly.

"Shit, baby. Just like that. Ahh…fuck."

As he moved his shirt out of the way, Ashley gave him a teasing look as she looked up at him. She truly enjoyed sucking his magnificent dick. The sense of control it gave her over him delighted her. As she lavished him with her mouthwatering dick-devotions, he was truly at her mercy.

She was fucked from behind as Ethan turned her over once more. She felt a sense of grounding as the table's cold marble pressed into her face. She pressed her hips back into him after he really fucked her hard, and she took him deep.

"Oh shit! Fuck! Fuck! Fuck! Please…please…" she cried out completely unaware of what exactly she was begging for.

She had converted into a cavernous vessel that was only there to submit and be assaulted by him. He used her dress to pull her closer to him and it sent her into a spasm. He swiftly removed it because it obstructed the path.

He finally turned her over onto her back and fucked her wildly once more as if she were invulnerable. He was almost there. So near. He slowed down and gawked as she arched her curvy back and kneaded herself, completely consumed in the sublime pleasure. He couldn't help himself. He pushed harder, then jerked out and covered her inner thigh and ass with his cum.

As he recovered his speaking ability, he gave her a kiss.

"Wow! That.Was.Incredible!"

Ethan still seemed awestruck by her. He fixed her gaze and gave her that contagious smile.

Ashley exclaimed, still out of breath, "We probably should join the party…"

He responded with a cheeky, suggestive look that suggested he had other ideas, "Erm, maybe yes…Or maybe not; I saw a wall over there, and I'd love to fuck your gorgeous body over it once I've recovered in about a few minutes."

Ashley wasn't complaining. She was all for it.

Chapter 4

The hard, cold pinch of the clamps on Ashley's nipples followed the cold metal chain resting on her stomach, causing her to shiver.

How she got there? Well, she and Ethan had decided to experiment with toys and spice things up a bit.

As blood surged from her hard nipples, her body quivered on the table. Her entire body was already on fire, despite the fact that she had barely been touched. Ethan slowly returned to the space between her legs. He kissed her lower stomach before bending his head forward. She sucked in a breath as his mouth found her inner lips after moving his hands over her inner thighs.

She moaned, "Oh, god."

Ashley had been told not to speak, and she was worried about the consequences. She was secure for the time being. Her clit was encircled in agonizing, harrowing movements as Ethan's tongue impaled her lips. Her whole body shook. In an effort to see what he was doing, she curled her head up and wrapped her fingers around the ropes that bound her wrists. With his lips and tongue on her pussy, Ethan was inside her, tasting, teasing, and torturing her.

She was loving every moment of it because it was everything she had ever fantasized about.

Like a powerful river seeking an outlet through her body, Ashley felt her first orgasm growing inside of her. Ethan allowed her climax to flow through her despite her fears that he would deny her this release. She could only hope that he would continue to delight her until the powerful climax could wash over her because her body was unable to move. She came quickly and pressed her hips firmly against his mouth. Ethan moved to her side and stroked her thighs, stomach, and breasts as her climax subsided. He lowered himself to face her. As the stubble of his neat beard brushed against her cheek, Ashley inhaled his musky, scent.

He pressed his fingers into her while staring directly into her eyes. Her back arched and she groaned. He gave her a firm nip and pushed her in as far as she could take it. Her muscles ached. Her toes and fingers flexed. She was experiencing a new orgasm. She clenched her jaw. Would he allow her to return?

She was not permitted to speak, nor was she permitted to raise her head to kiss him, despite her desperate desire for contact. Before beginning, they had established some guidelines.

She just couldn't stop herself.

She begged Ethan to touch her because she needed to be touched, whispering, "More."She feared that as soon as the words left her mouth, he would stop and leave her in such a tizzy state.

He ordered, "Say it again."

She begged, "More. Please, I want more."

He grinned.

He moved back between her legs after she dropped her head. However, he did not resume French kissing and mouth-teasing her. A buzzing sound made her heart skip a beat. As he moved a black wand over the delicate breast skin, she gasped. Ethan used the device to poke at her nipples, which were now burning because the clamps didn't have any blood in them. She had no idea that her nipples and breasts could become so sensitive. They stung with a longing to be released from the metal clamps that held them and pain. But she was aware that they wouldn't be let out.

Not yet.

The vibrator was moved between her legs. As he dragged the wand over her clit and thrust it between her lips, the harsh emotion nearly overpowered her. She wanted to cry out and beg him to stop but worried that if she did, he would respond by indeed stopping.

She did not wish for him to halt.

Never, not now.

As Ethan pushed the device into her, she felt her body shake. She put her legs apart. Her ankles pressed against the chains, pleading for release, but it was not granted. As she had been at the beginning, Ashley was still unable to move.

Ethan took the device out of her body. After returning to her side, he leaned down and gave her a kiss. She reciprocated his kiss without hesitation. She escaped with a grin. She was finally able to connect with her nemesis, which she had so desperately desired. After a second kiss, Ethan moved to free her ankles and wrists of their ties. As the blood slowly returned to her body, Ashley slowly moved her arms and legs. He then took the nipple clamps out. As the blood rushed to her nipples, she was shocked by the sweet sting of pleasure. As she slowly pushed herself up onto the table, she touched her breasts with her hands.

"What next?" she turned to look at Ethan.

Her need to be submissive had been satisfied. She had endured being completely helpless and being pushed to the edge multiple times while orgasming at his skilled hands and tongue over and over again. She now knew exactly what had to be done.

She had to do what she was good at.

Ethan's belt buckle was undone by Ashley as she leaned forward. After inserting her hand into his zipper, she took off his beautiful massive cock from his pants. She took him between her lips as she bent forward. As Ethan placed his hands on her back, she eagerly sucked him in and drew his cock close to her mouth. She smiled to herself as he gave a deep grunt. She took his entire length between her soft lips and sucked him harder.

She had a natural ability to delight others. She had thoroughly enjoyed the submission, but this was her favorite part. She turned to face him, spread her legs, and guided his cock inside of her as she did so. He swiftly entered her and wedged his shaft firmly in her. She yelled and curved her back, drawing him even closer to her. As he entered her, she sat back, giving him a perfect view.

The small, dim room heard her groans. The one light that was still shining down on the dark wood table where she had been tied and helpless moments earlier made her look up at the ceiling. She felt more in control and more like herself now that she could move her arms and body. As he continued to fuck her, she pushed herself up and gave him a kiss while tasting him. He moved faster and faster as he swung back and forth.

"Mmm…oh, Ethan!"

Her fantasy of being shackled was fulfilled. She only desired one thing at this point: to cum with his cock buried balls deep in her. She took his cock as deep as she could by putting her hips firmly against him. There were no ropes this time, so there was no concern that he would suddenly break free. Together, they were going to reach the end.

She let out a loud scream as she was tormented by his prodding, the pain, and the idea of being shackled and helpless. As her body burst into a final orgasm, her mind raced with all of it. Ethan left her alone. His warm sperm shot onto her skin as his cock exploded. Once more conscious of the wood table beneath her, the one she would never forget, she slowly lowered her body back down.

Ashley smiled deeply as Ethan cuddled her on the carpeted floor.

"That was amazing," she sighed.

"Yeah. Already planning what fantasy you want to explore next?" he asked.

"Hell yeah!"

Chapter 5

It was weekend and Ashley spent the previous night at Ethan's apartment. That night, she had a wet dream about him doing nasty things to her and woke up the following morning feeling extremely horny and in need of some hard dicking.

"Good morning," she heard him say from behind her, lightly kissing her neck.

"Mmm…morning."

He drew nearer to her. He gently pressed his torso against her back. After placing his chin on her shoulder, he gently turned her face so that it mirrored his by running his hand up the side of her face. Her lips were instantly attracted to his suppleness. His urgent but tender tongue entered her mouth almost immediately. They exchanged saliva and stroked each other's lips before melting into a passionate kiss. Ethan was skilled at kissing Ashley. This was what she liked, and he knew it.

He began to knead her breast as one of his hands slid into her nightie. As he rolled it between his fingers, Ashley's nipple became more solid.

"Ohh," she gasped.

Ethan continued to play with both of her breasts, much to her pleasure. Even more seductive was the fact that she had her back to him. She had to imagine his vivacious expression. That was a major motivator.

The tension quickly became excessive. She swung around and straddled him because she had to face him. She took control of the kiss as his hands barely left her breasts. Her craving for him grew stronger with each rotation of his tongue in her mouth. As he continued to stroke her breasts, she leaned back. When he added his mouth to the equation, she felt flutters in the base of her stomach as she carefully observed his hands move. With such lust, he licked and sucked on her nipples. As his desire for her bullet-like nubs coerced them to stand firmly in attention, a fire raged in the depths of her increasingly wet pussy. He moved with intent and yearning between the two breasts. It was tiring.

The tension was growing. Their tongues became entangled like laces as he pressed his soft lips against hers. She wished for more. That was how they played for a while.

His dick bobbed and bounced against her inner thigh beneath her. It appeared to be imploring for attention. She started by caressing him on the outside of his pants, and when his throbbing cock was ready to come out, she let him out of his pristine white shorts.

As her hand wrapped around his shaft and she began to jerk him off, their lips remained locked. He was smooth and thick. She wanted to try his taste. The silky outer layer of his pulsating meat enticed Ashley's tongue. She wanted to savor the sweetness of his tip at the back of her throat as much as she could.

She let her lips move up and down while holding the base of his cock. She was informed that he was pleased with her method by his throaty sighs of contentment. She took him deep, back-of-the-throat-tickling-tonsils deep every few strokes! He cherished it.

As she slid him in and out of her lips, Ashley would occasionally allow the fullness of her lips to apply some pressure as she danced her tongue delightfully around the head.

She confidently focused on him because Ethan liked it when she looked at him with her mouth full. She only turned her head away when she noticed how beautiful his fully erect manhood was or how his deep breathing affected his stomach. It was hypnotic!

She gently inserted each testicle one at a time into her mouth while running her tongue up and down his ball bag without letting her hand leave his shaft. He was so engrossed in ecstasy that he couldn't speak. His mouth was open. He eagerly awaited each passing moment as he continued.

As his pleasure became evident, she eventually began to taste his mild saltiness. She left as a result. She had such a juicy pussy. She was drenched.

One of Ashley's hands cupped a breast as he continued to jerk him off, and he began to groan.

She required more. She straddled him out of a desire to have her wetness acknowledged, so this time her ass was sixty-nine inches above his face. She lowered herself onto his eager mouth while he sat back. As his tongue touched her honey pot, joyous bolts shot through me. He immediately began to consume her nectar.

In order to get into a rhythm, Ethan held himself with both hands. To play with her clit, his taut tongue darted between her plump pussy lips before returning to her saturated hole. His tongue swung around her entrance, stopping only to lick both sides. While he kept his ever-hardening cock in her mouth, he was making fun of her. She put so much faith in it. She was giving him the best head ever while he was tongue-fucking her. It was so damn hot!

She would have screamed in a frantic manner each time he parted her lips and sunk his face into her if she hadn't had a full mouth of dick. She struggled, however, to remain present with her cock sucking when he turned his attention to her hardening love bud. She simply desired to let it out of her mouth and take pleasure in the sexy assault that was taking place between her legs.

He sucked and nibbled as well as flicked and licked. It was blissful bliss. As he devoured her aching snatch, Ashley's sighs of contentment grew in intensity.

She was forced to remove him from her mouth because he was eating. She needed some time to get lost in the exhilarating waves that were crashing against her. She gave him a deeper look into her by arching her back. Her essence ran down his chin and into his mouth. He took everything in. She was extremely open and soaking wet.

She wanted his full length and girth enclosed within my walls.

She could tell that Ethan also needed it. As usual, their chemistry was out of this world, and it became very clear that they needed to connect in a way that could only happen through penetration.

She turned to face him, lowered herself onto his dick, and angled herself above it. It was pure joy from the moment the head met the doorway to her warmth. Every single one of her nerves surfaced as her damp and inviting den was accessed by his beating dick.

She started to scream. In the most unplanned manner, their mouths connected, separated, and then reconnected. It was so incredibly sensual that it was almost awkward. His hand was on the small of her back, and she held her hands tightly around his neck as they moved together. Every time he moved up or down, his stiff dick slid against her embracing walls. A wave of effervescent ripples began to cascade down her back and bubble in her lower region as she slightly increased the pace. It was tasty.

Ethan eventually relaxed, and she soon found herself riding him up high like a sexy little cowgirl. She would occasionally lean forward, allow his dick to slip towards the mouth of her bleeding gash, and then slip back down until his unforgiving stiffness poked at her cervix once more. He gently urged her to take him deeper by placing his hand just above where her ass began to dip. She carried out exactly what he wanted in response to the subtle request. However, she required even more.

Ashley reached for the clitoral stimulator-equipped cock ring. As she gently rolled it down his length until it reached the base of his solid member, he eagerly watched. She changed her position and brought him back inside. The rubbery sensation of the clit stimulator quickly reached her tender hot spot. The stimulator's additional flavor took her to new heights as she rode him. She was overcome with excitement as she licked his mouth. The sensation was immense, so she continued to grind. Because it was hard for him to remain calm in the midst of everything that was going on, he kept grabbing at her thigh. The fact that Ethan was witnessing her exiting drove him absolutely insane.

He stood up after some time, which caused her to adjust again. Ashley found herself roughly in the same position as before after swinging each of my legs over his. She was straddling him, but this time the clit stimulator was present and ready to escalate the situation.

Ethan kept looking deeply into her eyes as she let the joy she was feeling take over me. She was completely at ease. She experienced an increase in all of her senses. As she moved back and forth on his dick, the bed linen's gentle rubbing against her leg added layer of sensuality and even the way her toes curled and interlocked contributed to the amazing sexual high.

Ethan had a full view of her excited pussy devouring him when she leaned back. He was in the front row. He was right there and saw everything. She felt him throb inside. She remained in that position and continued to grind on him because he clearly liked what he saw.

The intense pain of an orgasm surfaced as her pleasure grew. It was the distance to reach. She could practically taste the sweetness. She continued to thrust back and forth, occasionally taking him again after bringing him all the way out. More than she was playing with him, she was making fun of herself.

Ashley's cervix contracted, and she had a lot of juice. She was extremely agitated and sticky. Ethan occasionally gently added additional thrusts to her grinding. She was brought ever so slightly closer by each person. Until she was ready to spill, she continued to let him slide inside of her. She experienced a surge of fulfillment as a bubbling sensation and the pressure of her satisfaction burst through. She covered his entire cock. His response was to turn her on her back, pull her legs apart, and penetrate her in a missionary manner. In that position, the stimulator on his cock ring performed even better. The rubber stimulator's flexibility rubbed up the entire length of her straight clitoris with each thrust.

He seized the opportunity to entice her with his cock. He would enter slowly, exit quickly, pause for a moment or two, and then repeat. She was unsure of how much more she could physically take due to the anticipation of how he felt inside her and the additional sensation provided by the sex toy. Her previous orgasm was still having an effect on her body, which was weak from all the pleasure it had received. She wouldn't let go of that old desire to cum again.

She was done for when Ethan threw one of her legs back. He tried to kiss Ashley, but she was barely there when she found herself once more on the verge. She simply could not! Her face and body were shaken violently by ecstasy.

He continued to dick her with the same tenacity and much greater passion as a dog on heat. As he continued to fuck her up, he eventually let a little of his body weight rest on her. Her wet snatch dribbled even more as a result of the bonus of him being on top of her. Ashley's cunt was swollen, juicy, and covered in water. He was aware that she was about to blow again. He kept doing the same thing until the pressure of her orgasm subsided.

Ethan backed out and sat back on his heels as he observed her panting in the midst of her elation. As he had anticipated, she had finished with the cock ring, so he removed it. He was accurate. Her clit could not take any more, despite the fact that it was amusing. He entered her without the ring as she continued to watch, her pussy tingling like crazy. She was extremely sensitive, but it wasn't too bad. In point of fact, he chose a lovely pace. Her intense spasms were perfectly complemented by his internal massage.

As she kept her legs spread as wide as they could be, Ethan found a new rhythm. He took control of her body at that point. He could fuck her at any speed or intensity he wanted because she was his.

She let her hand slip between her legs as his strokes worked their magic, and two of my fingers found her throbbing clit. As Ethan's dick moved in and out, she gently rubbed on it.

This time, the pressure came from beneath her cervix. The sudden need to pee was enormous. She let out an enormous gusher without much warning. She went over and over him. He wanted it that way!

Their lips once more locked, but only for a brief moment.

"Do you intend to come for me?" Through her pants and deep breaths, she asked him.

He responded by striking her with deep thrusts that slapped his balls against her. His focus was fixed on hers. He was on his way, and he was about to arrive.

He let out guttural groans with each strike as he got closer. He was unable to contain the brewing storm. His desire was getting ready to explode. After a few more pumps, his eruption sent her flying. As he gave in to his ecstasy, his body became less rigid.

He had completely relaxed in a matter of seconds, and his tongue entered her mouth. He enjoyed the electricity coursing through his limbs as they shared a tender kiss.

Chapter 6

"When was the most recent time you were truly fucked in a hotel?" In response, Ashley's cheeks burned. In fact, Ethan was asking this question in a coffee shop? She wondered if anyone could hear the filth coming from his mouth as she looked around. What a lovely mouth! She wanted to suck and bite Ethan's bottom lip because it was so pouty.

They were at the moment in Paris. She had sought permission from her boss because Ethan wanted to take a vacation and had a week off from work–more like Ethan had used his power as a multi-billionaire to get her off work.

Although he had been extremely persuasive, Ashley had initially refused to go. Ethan was always able to obtain whatever he desired.

"Answer me."He narrowed his eyes, creating a crease in the corners.

She took a breath. "Months."

His succulent lips parted in a conspiratorial smirk, the edge of which was raised. She held her thighs together tightly.

He stood, grabbed his coat, and tossed a fifty into the table after opening his wallet. "Let's go."

"Where are we headed?" She followed him even as the question lingered in the air without a response.

Once outside, he took her hand in his. "Returning to the hotel."

The night sparkled all around as street lights reflected in still puddles. Although the café was only a few blocks away from their hotel, he pulled her inside when the elevator opened and her heart raced. Before his mouth smashed into hers, she barely had time to think. Crude and imposing. Her heart rate increased as well as slowed.

A whimper erupted as his tongue slipped along hers. A dim hallway opened up when the elevator opened. He led her out and then lifted her after pushing her against a wall. His waist was covered in legs. They hadn't even entered their hotel room yet, and her cunt was hurting. She couldn't stop talking about him. When they finally reached the room, he pinned her wrists against the door's back.

He smiled wickedly and then took her lips once more without speaking. Her skin became numb. She yearned for every moment of it, though she had no idea what he had in store for her. After sucking on her neck, he let go of her arms. She took the chance by removing his coat from his shoulder and allowing it to fall to the ground. He then followed suit.

The enticing sound of a zipper falling filled the small space after he unbuckled her belt. He probed her aching clit all the way down to the edge of her stomach, just below her belly button. She let him into her body. As his fingers found her slick slit, she whimpered.

"You can't have it, though I know you want it.No, not yet." He spoke in a deep, breathy voice.

His other hand found her opening and invaded without delay after he fisted the back of her head.

As he fingerfucked her, she clung to his shirt and opened her mouth before he pinned her hands over her head and held them there. Her body was scuffed by his touch. Caressing. Appraising. Claiming. It moved downward and once more entered her folds. He took in her groans like food.

Before torturing her, he slipped his fingers into her mouth and teased her tongue. You always have the best flavor.

She needed to be abused, taken advantage of, and made to whine like the deep-seated whore she was deep down. As if he owned them and were fueled by them, he ate her sounds. He also did. His hands moved throughout her body. His tongue was infatuated with her mouth. She was filled with the girth of his fingers, getting ready for what she prayed would happen.

He grabbed her by the throat."Those who wait will reap the benefits. Do you not wish to be good for me?"

"I want to be good for you, daddy," she said, nodding.

He continued his assault on her cunt and fixed his gaze on her. She got even wetter when he didn't say anything or just stared at her. It was so ominous that it was almost predatory.

She begged, "Please," but she had no idea why. For him to halt? Give her more? Both? She wasn't even sure she knew who she was anymore.

He silently marked his territory by drawing his tongue over her open mouth. She felt such strong desires and needs surge through her. He then halted. Her attention was immediately drawn to the rhythm of her clit in the silence. Like a tiny heart that longed for him.

Ethan walked her backwards into their room and pinned her against a wall once more as he turned the corner. He skillfully stroked her mouth's warm cavern with his tongue. His hand went back around her throat abruptly. Her jaw opened. As he turned on the light, he saw her cruel face.

"You require this." Her lips were devoured by his. "You have a tiny cunt that deserves to be fucked by daddy."

He pushed her forward onto a sofa, knelt behind her, and caressed her underarms. As he worked her panties and jeans down, she watched over her shoulder.

The warmth of his kisses on her cheeks quickly dampened the air that was licking at her slit. It was a sight to behold when he appeared. He had his eyes closed. As he caressed her plumpness with his face, he moved like a man lost in reverent worship as he gripped her thighs. He reached up and pressed her shoulders into the back of the sofa, arching her as his tongue slipped between her creases. Despite her fluttering eyes, she was able to focus on him once more. Her honeyed goodness was exposed to him in his large hands as he held her open.

Before taking a long, slow lick and repeating the depravity, he spit on her pussy. She was discovering that she liked him because of this. Such a sophisticated person with lingering lascivious tastes beneath his refined exterior. Someone who was able to satisfy all of her requirements and even arouse new ones.

As he ate her, the tip of his nose moved across her groin. She groaned. She imagined what it would be like for him to fuck her there as she gripped the sofa's back. Ethan was free to do whatever he wanted. Everything about her. Evety gap. With his expertise, he had earned it.

He continued eating until her screams became more audible, forcing air out of the small room. As her climax swept through her stomach and melted from her cunt, she held onto his hand. However, his attacks never stopped. He knelt next to her on the sofa, fucking her incessantly while effortlessly pressing his fingers into her wet entrance.

"You don't even want to think about anything anymore, do you?" His breath hit her face hard.

Stars shot out of her eyes as she shook her head. "No, daddy."

He was accurate. She had wanted to be in such bliss that she couldn't speak or think and that he would make all decisions on his own. She was just a plaything. Something to be toyed with and enjoyed.

Despite the fact that her cunt squeezed his fingers in release, he continued to grip her throat. He wanted it all. As soon as he stood to undo his belt and zipper, his intensity decreased. He quickly slipped into her like a glove made to perfection.

As he ripped her blouse open and then engulfed her breasts with his large hands, buttons popped and scattered across the floor. After he left, how could she ever go back to anyone else? After how he'd worshipped her body for the past few months.

She repositioned herself and felt his weight force her to open. Her hard nipples were teased and brushed by her long hair. His fingers dug into her hips' flesh.

"You feel so good!"

She felt the warmth of that praise radiating through her. She regained control and, desperate for more, pushed her ass back onto his cock.

"Baby, just like that. Fuck daddy like you're on a mission." By ghosting over her nipples and stroking her throat, he praised her. After that, he used her torn blouse to lift and turn her before putting her back on the couch. He said, referring to her arms, "Keep them behind you." He stood with his enormous cock protruding like a creamy treat.

"Good girl."

He lowered her and cupped the back of her head. To taste herself on him, she happily opened her mouth. As she took her first lick, a moan resonated throughout his thickness. He moved his hips hard. He made such sexy sounds. They soon settled into a rhythm together before he grabbed her hair and pulled her back. She raised her eyes to meet his. Her mouth corner dripped with drool.

His dick's head was traced around her swollen lips by him.

"You like to mess up, don't you?"

He kissed her after kneeling once more and squeezing the sides of her head into his willing mouth. Making love in their own unique way, they slid their tongues against one another.

"Baby girl, I'm far from finished with you."As he held her by the neck, he caressed her chest with his experienced hands, rubbing the beads in her nipples with his palms.

"I never want you to be," she said.

He kissed her with every ounce of passion after giving her a rich and deep laugh. He had a nipple between his fingers. Her lower lip was caught between his teeth. He put pressure on them both, which led to a desperate gasp. She never desired to be free because she was like a fly caught in his web. She desired to be used, eaten, and devoured.

He got back to his feet and stepped back into her, towering over her. As he used her mouth, spit fell down his dick. She felt so used because of his size, which filled her throat. He would stop and kiss her, as if to express gratitude, before fucking her face once more, giving her a sense of respect and beauty. He and she were only made more enraged by the gurgling sounds.

"You're doing a great job." He gave her cheek a rub.

He quickly got her completely undressed. He pulled her body down and hooked his arms under her thighs, positioning her for future use, to which she stared in anticipation and awe. Her thighs were wide apart. She encircled his slick, fiery cock with one hand. His hands once more settled into her. She had never experienced passion that consumed her so completely. He was obsessed with her. His ferocity was almost too much to bear. However, excitement won out.

In an act of dominance, he forced the honey into her mouth after sucking it from his fingers. She felt so desired and desired by something so crudely filthy. Despite her confusion, she never wanted it to end. She was forced to focus on him as his free hand pinned her head back.

"Cum for me."

As he returned to work, stroking her cunt like a master, their lips met once more. Despite her best efforts to please him, waves kept crashing over her body and stilling her hand.

Her pelvis began to ache sweetly and warmly. As she approached and soaked his palm, uncontrollable wetness squirted forward.

"A nice girl."Before kneeling and sucking the lust from its source, he praised. "Let it go."She was forever suspended in orgasm as he ate up her folds with his tongue.

She was in shock as he got back up and stroked her spot with his fingers. He groped her hard with force. Her eyes rolled. Her entire body shook as she squirmed once more. It seemed as though he had taken control of her inside and made her his. Her skin felt sensitive everywhere. As he pulled her into his arms and rotated them so that he rested on the sofa, their tongues interacted with each other's mouths.

Writhing like a luring nymph, she straddled his lap and ground her pussy along his length. She pleaded, "Please."His fingers had been amazing, but her body wanted more substance in them. She only lifted enough for him to pull his jeans down.

"Kindly fuck me, daddy."

"Show me." As she sank down and embraced his dick, he stared up at her, almost challenging her. "Show me what a nasty girl you are."

Before landing on him, she grabbed the back of the small couch and rolled her hips a few times. He perfectly stuffed her. Just enough to the point where the pleasure of the stretch clashed with the pain. She could feel every vein in his naked body. He pushed her forward by pressing his fingertips into her hips and then her ass. Between them, there were moans.

"There you go, fuck me, baby," he said.

She groaned at the gravelly sexiness in his voice. His lips moved with his breaths. His grip extended her, and air licked her groin. She had to, had to keep this going. She rode him hard, pressing her weight against his firm chest. Her body boiled over with the night's frantic energy. She screamed as he squeezed her nipples. He joined her in groans, which got louder. She debated whether she desired another climax at this point.

He pinned her arms behind her back after grabbing her throat. She never stopped sexing him. As she pressed her clit against his pelvis, her groans got louder. Her body swung. Before dipping her head to kiss him, she felt unsteady and braced herself against his chest. She then moved slowly atop him to make the climax last.

She needed more, though. Nothing would ever suffice. As she dug deeper into his slick cock, she arched her back.

"Yes, you are still starving, aren't you?" He laughed. "Do you want me to fuck you hard with my cock?"

"Yes, daddy.Yes, oh my god. Use me. Destroy me. Make me useless to everyone else."

He rolled his hips and lifted with soft thrusts to respond to her movements. His breath hit her breasts hard. His pants got louder. She took the reins and rode him more quickly.

"Come on, come on," he persuaded her.

She came so many times she lost count, but her pulsating cunt was enough to send him over the edge. She became still as his warm cum filled her. He sucked her nipple, eagerly tracing it with his tongue, as she held him close.

"You look so stunning like this, even when you're cock drunk and exhausted."

She laughed softly and whispered, "That was fucking amazing," causing his cock to recede. She adored the sensation of cum coming out of her.

With a gentleness that threatened to break her more than his rough fucking ever could, he cradled her in his arms and drew his fingertips over her back and the peaks of her shoulder blades. He left behind a trail of goosebumps. The afterglow was delicate and soft despite how ferociously he had had her. She had required a man who could do both.

After a brief pause of silence, he finally spoke, "I love doing this with you."

Her cheeks felt a rush of fresh heat. She was extremely touched by receiving such tender treatment. She turned her head to face him. "Yeah?"

His eyes were filled with a smile that tugged at his lips. "Yeah."He stroked her cheek with the back of his hand. "I'll order some food for us."

She guffawed. "That would be nice. Maybe a shower first?"

"Whatever you want."She felt a slight tremble as he brushed her shoulder hair. "You can have it."

"I hope there are seconds in that."She brushed her bottom lip with her teeth. "Tonight, I'm a greedy girl."

His eyes were lit up by his smile. "Good. That is my preferred variety."

Her heart soared. Fuck!She was in love with him.

Chapter 7

In the weeks that followed, Ashley and Ethan maintained their usual routine of fucking each other. Sometimes, they fucked like animals on heat, and other times they went slow, making love to each other's bodies. Ashley thought about how fucked she was for falling in love with Ethan as she landed at the airport. She had been gone for a week. It had been a business trip with her boss and while she was away, she missed Ethan. Which was why she went straight to his penthouse once she arrived.

It was still early in the morning and he was asleep. She stripped herself of the dress she was wearing and joined him in bed. He stirred.

She felt a jolt of excitement run through her. He would soon discover that she was back as he was awakening. Ashley didn't want to wake Ethan up and ruin the magic of the surprise, so she lightly brushed her lips across his cheek and down to his mouth. She matched his gaze, enjoying the pleasure she felt as she watched his handsome features change. As her hand swiftly moved up and down his throbbing cock, his jaw jerked back to face her, and his tongue parted in an attempt to taste her mouth once more.

She instinctively reached out to stroke his cock beneath the crisp cotton sheet as her entire body throbbed. She heard his breath catch at the sight of her, and she saw his eyes flash as she did so—he had noticed the camisole she was wearing. With a smug smile, she sat back and ran her hands across her chest, delighting in the feeling of his palm finally pressing against her skin after so long. Through the black lace, she could see that he was enticed by her body and was drawn to it. She gently ran her fingers under the cami's straps, pressing her boobs against the cups that held them in place. She wanted to make fun of him, hoping that he would long for her as much as she had for him. Ethan was able to see her silky breasts after Ashley removed the cups. He wetted her cleavage and sucked on one of her hardening boobs as she lustfully pulled at the tingling globes. He took it with a firm grip and nuzzled it as his hungry tongue moved quickly from one tit to the other. As he sucked almost her entire breast into his mouth, she reveled in how starved he was for her by playing with his hair. Ethan raised his head to her mouth once more, kissing her deeply and urgently, as if he had read her mind. Finally, she was with him, and she could touch, smell, and taste him.

She couldn't wait to take his pulsing shaft in her hand as soon as he lifted the sheet just a little to show her his already rigid cock. He held her neck to his lips, ran a hand up her back, and yanked the cami up with it as she began to work it under the sheets. Over her now-exposed butt, electricity shot down her spine. Her body struggled to contain the delightful sensations she was feeling as it gyrated and rocked. She wanted to be drunk. Both her and Ethan's cock were objects of worship for Ashley.

As she jerked him off, he chuckled as he fixed her and gently slid the foreskin over his cock and back to feel the veins that connected his stuffed tool. She matched his gaze, enjoying the pleasure she felt as she watched his handsome features change. As her hand swiftly moved up and down his throbbing cock, his jaw jerked back to face her, and his tongue parted in an endeavor to savor her mouth once more.

After that, he made a brief movement away from her. She spread her legs over him as he sat back on his heels and found her tits once more as he sat up and held her close. Now, wholly intoxicated by his insistent tongue, hard body, and thick cock, she was screaming deliriously. She felt as though she would never be able to stop kissing him as his mouth met hers once more. When he took hold of her thighs and swept her onto her back in the crumpled sheets, she sighed with pleasure because she had completely given in to his sexual power.

She now felt a sensation of warmth crackle through her. Those days of fingering herself, playing with her own tits, and using a variety of different toys and vibrators had been so much fun, especially if he had been online with her, but nothing could have prepared her for the sensation of his skin on hers after a whole seven days. The way his mouth stroked her snatch. The happiness Ashley experienced as Ethan spread her legs wide was a sign that she was frantic for it to occur immediately. His tongue opened her and flicked up to the hot nib of her clit as he kissed and nibbled the soft insides of her thigh, pushing the gusset of her panties away to expose her pussy and kissing the lips there as passionately as he did her mouth. To prevent herself from exploding, she clenched her fists on the sheet. As she tried not to orgasm, she saw him raise his head to look right into her eyes, his own smoldering with purpose. Ethan drew the flat expanse of his tongue along the length of her dewy pussy, now taunting her back.

Once.

Ashley threw her head back in elation as her pussy wobbled in white-hot need and he swam inside her, licking her lips and slit so he could taste every part of her.

She worked her way through his long, black hair with her hand. She adored what he was doing to her and loved him so much. As he ate her greedily, she gasped in delight and stroked one of her thick nipples.

After dreaming about the pussy licking for so long on the plane, she wanted to watch it all, but it was almost too much.

She lay back, hot and breathless, riding wave after wave of bliss, knowing that he would raise his eyes to look at her. He had told her a lot of times that he loved seeing how she responded to him and that he always wanted to make sure he was making her as interested as possible.

She felt his hand reaching up to her writhing body as she closed her eyes in ecstasy. She eagerly parted her lips as two strong fingers gently pressed against them, bringing them into her mouth and sucking them in like she was thirsty. After slowly and enticingly pushing them in and out, he abruptly whipped them away from her suckling lips and sucked them deep inside her. Her slick pussy was now wet from her own mouth and her trembling hole, and she mewled with lustful delight.

Just as she had done to herself numerous times while she was away, he began to finger-fuck her, but he was so much better at it than she was. As he worked her into a spasm with his mouth wide open, tongue outstretched, and lips glistening and shining with her pussy juice, he was licking her while his fingers were moving in and out of her.

She rode his tongue, her tits wobbling as she arched into an orgasm, her naked lust driving her on. He reached up to cup her breasts as she came hard, her hips buckling up to his mouth, and Ethan's focus was always on her snatching motion. As the last of her orgasm subsided, she felt him move up her body to kiss her once more. She enjoyed the taste of her pussy on his lips and the addictive attraction between their mouths. He laid back on the bed and dragged Ashley with him. She kissed down his body until she reached his cock with a loose, languid smile. She was more than happy to oblige, rubbing and sucking when she saw him prop himself up on his elbows out of the corner of her eye so he could watch her work on him. As she sucked his shaft deeply into her mouth, his strong hand gently pushed her hair from her face. She took in the smell, feel, and sound of his voice—his gasps and moans—between her lips. She loved trying to suck as much of him down her throat as she could, increasing the rhythm, depth, and speed, and turning herself on as much as she did him because he had always been too big for her to fully swallow.

She moved her mouth away from Ethan's cock and smiled coquettishly at him before turning away from him to show him her pussy. She needed to feel him in her pussy, so they moaned together as he slid his thick cock deep inside as he tenderly ran a hand over one of her smooth buttocks and his mouth followed.

When she sneaked a glance behind her, she was delighted by how he felt and how he looked. She could feel her tits shimmy with each slap of his hips against her buttocks as Ethan fucked her, his shaft effortlessly entering and exiting her, slick, thick, and hitting her spot. They lost themselves in the process of finding one another as each thrust lifted her higher to a location that only they knew.

When Ethan was inside Ashley, she lost all sense and thought. She was only aware of their bodies moving together in the hottest sex she had ever experienced while he was fucking her. She wanted to come and wanted it to continue forever.

Ethan slid his grateful hands over Ashley's burning skin as his body stretched out along her back. She was enthralled by his pelvis's skillful circling away from her, followed by the sensation of his palms resting against her sodden vulva, pushing her hair away from her neck with his fingers and placing his wet mouth on her shoulders and the back of her neck. He felt and smelled incredible. Sex sweat and desire were mixed with a faint scent of body wash. She had been waiting for this all along. Everything.

He grabbed her hard and now held her down, controlling her body. She reached out to him in a horny delirium, moaning, and he took her thin hand and kissed her lovingly but did not stop the fuck. Now, her pussy was undulating and milking his cock with each stroke. She could feel her speeding toward the place where everything in her melted and exploded at the same time. Her pussy was getting tighter, but her body wanted more. His cock circling, thrusting, and having her, she could hear him moan from somewhere behind her. As if he wanted this increasingly frantic moment to show her how much he missed her and how much he craved every inch of her body, the fuck's intensity seemed to express something from within him to her. He was also determined to show her with his hands and mouth this morning. using his cock.

He was repeatedly slamming his prick inside her and relentlessly sliding in and out while Ashley was gasping and trying so hard to hold on. The thought made her pussy tremble and her breath speed up even more as she imagined how his firm shaft would be glistening with her juice right then. She gave herself over to being completely controlled by his beautiful cock, jettisoned to the location where there was nothing but shards of starlight and vast, endless waves of pleasure and release. The louder she got, the more she could feel him pushing his hips against her even faster and harder.

He deeply sighed as they reclined against the pillows and he wrapped her in his strong arms. She congratulated herself on the surprise as she felt a trickle of spunk run down her thigh, just like the water had in the bathroom earlier.

"Good morning," Ethan murmured against her temple. "I missed you."

"I missed you too."

Ethan stared at her which such intensity that it scared her.

"I love you, Ashley," he finally said and she froze for a millisecond. Her heart soared like a bat out of hell. He loved her too. He reciprocated her feelings for him.

"I love you too, Ethan," she said, her voice barely a whisper.

Ashley curled up into his chest and softened into sleep with a smile on her lips. She was home.

Chapter 8

Ethan couldn't believe it.

Ashley was stunning. She was so stunning that Ethan sometimes found it hard to believe she had agreed to spend the rest of her life with him. He used to sneak a peek at her when she wasn't looking—the way she pouted when she was concentrating on something, the way her eyes twinkled when she laughed, and the graceful curve of her neck. Her calf. Those succulent breasts.

Also, he didn't miss the way Ashley looked at his naked body—that alluring combination of admiration and desire, her eyes running down his thighs, up his strong arms, and back up to linger on his cock. Her gaze would move over his skin like fingers.

His cock began to bleed as a result of the thought.

As he cuddled into her back, he sighed to himself, "I need you."

He was enthralled by the sensation of her naked flesh against his own.

"I should feel you. I need to fuck you."

His mouth became moist with desire as soon as his lips touched her neck. He placed a hand on her mound by sliding it under the sheet.

He planted kiss after kiss on her silky skin as Ashley's hand reached up to cradle his head.

She then began to turn away once more. Ethan held onto her because he was so desperate for her and couldn't let go now that she was awake. However, she was only turning on the bedside light when she returned to him and gave him passionate kisses.

He slipped his tongue deep into her mouth and enjoyed the closeness as they delicately but intently stroked each other with their fingers entwined. He moved his hand over one of her full breasts, and squeezed it hard, enjoying the soft flesh and her nipple stiffening against his palm.

Ethan could touch Ashley wherever he wanted as she rolled to face him with her body open and ready. He was completely focused on the stunning woman who was wrapped in the sheets beneath him, and the argument vanished once more from his thoughts.

She gave a satisfied sigh.

Ethan pushed the sheet away from her torso, wanting to see and feel more of her, ferried by the sound of her breath caressing the air. As he removed the cotton from her skin, she instinctively opened her thighs. She arched her back in satisfaction and kept her gaze fixed on him as he sucked one of her boobs into his mouth with ferocity.

As they resumed their kissing, she let out a moan, and she responded so quickly that his body pounded with need. Within the firmness of their loving embrace, their bodies easily moved together.

He moved his hand over her. Cupping her so he could eat her tits once more as he glid between her breasts, down her body to her mound, and back up. When they got close, got naked, and put their mouths on each other, he could feel the merging, the melting together in flame-red passion. They were two unique bodies combined into a single, vast, and overpowering sexual desire.

As he moved down the bed, Ashley pushed the sheets away from her. They were two individuals moving together with a single objective—to place Ethan's head between their thighs.

He cradled one of her lean legs over his shoulder as he buried his mouth in her moist labia because he didn't want to move his hand from her body and break the connection.

He imagined she was watching him as he flicked his tongue against her delectable shaved pussy with her hand in his hair, her fingers twisting and pulling him closer to her. Knowing that she had always enjoyed watching him snog her cunt, lapping deeply at her sweet, musky essence, the thought made him harder. As she smoothed her palm over his head and stroked it as she writhed against the sheets and against his soaking mouth, she tasted so good that waves of bliss broke over his body.

Ethan noticed as she was moaning that she was handling her own breast, pulling at her nipple, and teasing herself even more as she pulled and wobbled at her straining flesh. Ethan glanced up to see her.

Ethan dug even deeper, inserting his tongue completely inside her and swirling and probing. He looked up at her, wanting to see how happy she was on her face, in her closed eyes, and her mouth that was parted. His cock was getting even thicker as he watched her enslaved by her lust and his shaft was pressing against the sheets.

He wanted to make her feel even better. He slid two thick fingers into her and rotated them in her dripping hole in a tantalizing way. As he finger-fucked her more quickly, his tongue danced teasingly over her hard clitoris. When he looked up, he saw her throwing her head back in euphoria, and he grunted with joy.

Ethan sat up and nurtured her supple body, pussy in both mouth and chin. He could see how wide her legs were. Desire blazed in her eyes. He drew her closer to him, threw another leg over his shoulder, and slid his cock deep into her warm, wet hole. She firmly took hold of his shaft to welcome him home. Every sigh that came out of her parted lips made him work harder and more determined to get every square inch of her. He moved slowly and made insistent thrusts.

Their mouths were once more locked as he lay against her. Even though he was fucking her faster and faster and rubbing her harder and harder, their kissing was so tender and loving. He loved fucking Ashley, and he especially liked fucking her this way, the way she liked it. After that, he fell to the bed, longing for Ashley to feel the full force of his big dick inside her.

The bed creaked beneath them as they unrestrainedly fucked as he took her hard and rode her quickly.

He reached out to kiss her once more, overcome by an overwhelming desire to hold her close. He felt that being close to her either calmed him down or greatly exhilarated him, and both of those feelings were pulling at his soul and body tonight. Her embrace was an oasis for his frazzled mind and a salve for his troubled heart. Any time he needed to, he could stretch out and be vulnerable with her, and be held by her. He loved the fact that love held the roaring, crackling sex between them. He adored her. Lust reached a new high as the waves of love rose between them.

Now that they were on all fours, Ethan slammed into her with ease, her pussy walls sucking him in and milking his cock. The pleasure was returning. Ashley mewled as she glanced back to observe his pelvis moving and smacking against her gyrating buttocks, and Ethan was gasping for air.

He slowed down and returned to her neck and mouth, sampling her kisses. His cock had other ideas, and he had no choice but to follow them. He didn't want this moment to end, the connection to end.

He pulled her up hard. As she squirmed against him, Ashley was crying even louder and tossing her hair. He brought her back to him once more and briefly kissed her neck, but the fuck had taken control of both of them. As she clasped her hips to him and reached behind her for his hand, she tethered love and lust together and held him there as he pounded into and out of her.

He observed her arched her back in pleasure and bit her lip in an effort to contain his cock, but he was determined to have her in as many positions as she could take before he burst.

He emerged from her and collapsed on his back, his chest rising. Ashley took hold of his thick cock. He could see that she was enjoying the fact that she could taste both of them simultaneously, just like he was, as she closed her wet mouth around it. His chest was massaged by her free hand. She had to be able to feel how hard her tongue was making him and how hard his heart was beating.

Ethan thought that she was an expert at blowjobs as he moved his tongue across his lips before they parted in pleasure.

He put his head up. The sound of her hungry lips smacking as she sucked him pushed him further and further to the point of no return, despite his desire to observe her.

Ashley swung her dripping tongue over his glistening glans while moaning deliriously as she enthusiastically lapped him from balls to tip.Ethan had to use all of his strength not to immediately burst into her mouth.

She moved over him and her body melted against his, letting his cock fall stiffly against his belly. Ethan got to enjoy the flavor of both of them in his mouth this time as she kissed him with her lips pressed to his.

As his length stretched her wet hole, Ashley mounted him once more, gasping for air. He nuzzled and clutched her ass as he held her hips to him. He had no choice but to keep her there and not let her go. She skidded energetically up and down his shaft, dampening him with her juices, her ass cheeks parted in his hands.

She reached back and touched her skin with one of his hands. She had frequently told Ethan that she adored the feeling of being open while she was simultaneously drilled with his cock, and he was aware of her desire for him to spread her ass as far as it could go. He accepted with pleasure. Even though securing her to his prick by her parted cheeks turned him on just as much, if not more, he would never deny her any pleasure he could provide.

As she writhed and jiggled her breasts in front of him, he couldn't stop staring at her. His lust was so severe that he pulled Ashley's hands to his chest, relying on the pressure on his rib cage to control his hip grinding. To give in to everything, including the smell of their sex, the sounds she made, the sight of her body swaying and swiveling on top of him, and the sensation of her hot, wet pussy as she rode his cock into sexual oblivion, he needed her to hold him, ground him, and hold him.

Ashley knew so much about Ethan's body. For them to hold hands once more, she slowed down her motions and brought her body closer to his. As he knew he would, he was willingly enslaved by her, relinquishing himself in her, and he treasured the time they had spent together.

However, she was now arching her head back and enjoying herself on his cock. Leaning back, she let him do some of the work while she assisted herself by pressing her palms into his firm thighs. The ease with which she could take the thickness of his penis, Ethan thought to himself, God. She had grown accustomed to him over the years and was now able to take him in and eat him, dribbling all over him as she slid effortlessly up and down his shaft. As he fucked her once more, her breasts started to bounce back in front of him, and he eagerly grabbed them up. He manipulated the flesh and teased her nipples, which were getting tighter with each stroke.

He knew Ashley was getting close because of her stiffening tits and the way her slick pussy was milking his cock. She grabbed his hands to her hips and placed hers on top as he bounced her up and down on his hard prick. By holding him there, she made sure that every part of their bodies became a sensual bond of love and desire. Then she came, her body stretched into her release, and she moaned heavily. Ethan nearly fell as he watched her scream in hysterics as wave after wave of pleasure consumed her body, his pelvis still grinding against hers.

She gave up and fell on him. While he was still gently moving inside her, he lovingly kissed her until she stopped having orgasms. Desire was ever-present as they stared into each other's eyes, their communication now crystal clear. As they held hands, he sucked one of Ashley's tits into his mouth and sank his shaft as far into her as it could go. He fucked her hard and fast, and before he knew it, he was coming too.

As the room swung away from him, his hips were jerking and he was ramming hot cum into her cunt. Her pussy, hot and wet, wrapped around his pulsating penis, was all that remained for him at this point. Nobody else existed, and nothing else amounted to something. They were the only ones there.

As he dismounted, Ethan spilled cum onto his belly. As she swept her hair over her shoulder, she stroked his face and pressed against his chest before standing up and moving away from him.

He quietly murmured to her, "I really missed this."

After giving him a long, long kiss that made him feel both happy and relieved, she got out of the bed and went to the bathroom.

As the sweet relief of sleep gently fell upon him, he smiled as he watched her leave.

They were always going to be together forever.

Also by Amber Dickson

Nasty Daddy
Adrian Richardson isn't just older...
He's her stepbrother..
And a very hot and downright sexy one at that.

Fiona Jones hates that she has to move in with her mother's new family. But when her mother and her new husband go on their honeymoon trip, she is left under the custody of her dangerously sexy English accented stepbrother.

Fiona finally gets what she's always wanted. A Nasty Daddy.

This is a Steamy Short Story Romance. No Cliffhangers. If you love short romances with steamy sex scenes and a happily ever after, then you'll absolutely love this book and find it worthwhile